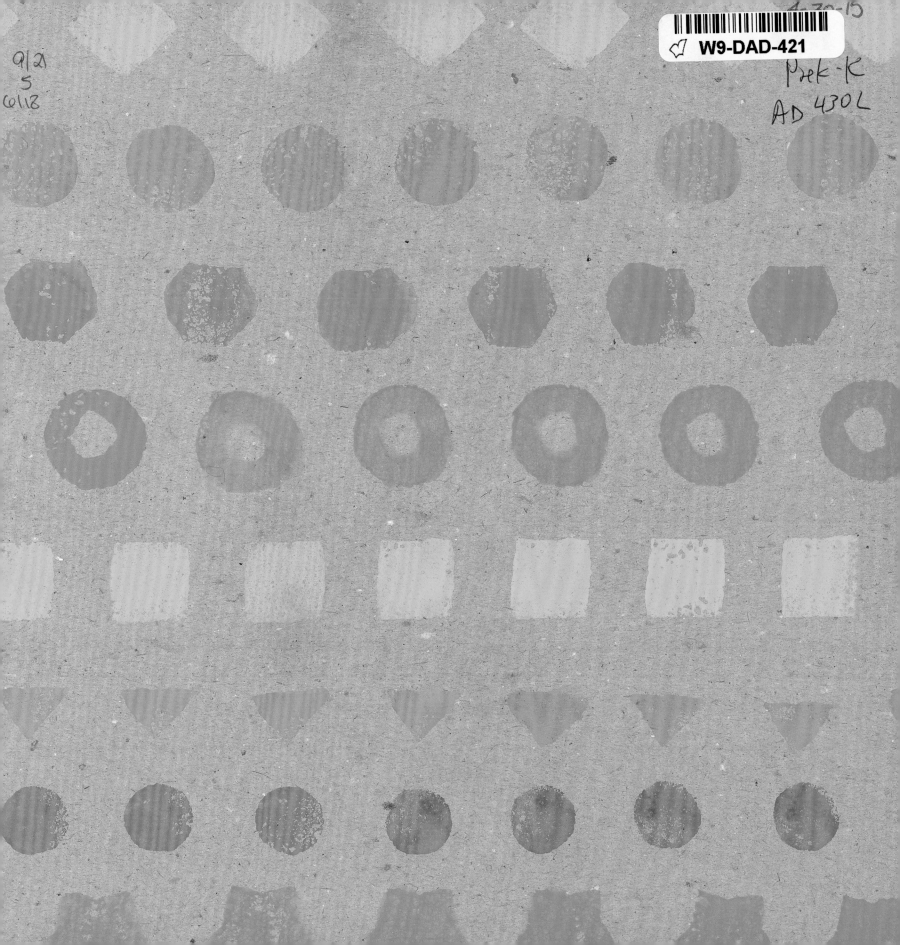
W9-DAD-421

This picture book helps children learn about mathematical concepts through a colorful and entertaining story.

Math concepts explored may include:
• Understanding math concepts
• Shape and space
• Explaining the basic concept of space and three types of plane figures: triangle, quadrangle (tetragon), circle

About the Author
Hee-jung Chang majored in psychology at Ewha Womans University in Seoul, South Korea, and studied developmental psychology at the university's graduate school. An active member of a children's book group for professional authors, Hee-jung has written many books for children.

About the Illustrator
Sung-hwa Chung majored in visual design in high school and in college. She won an award at the Korean Andersen Drawing Contest, and she was a runner up at Noma Concours in 2004.

TanTan Math Story *"Could You Lift Up Your Bottom?"*

Original Korean edition © Yeowon Media Co., Ltd

This U.S edition published in 2015 by TANTAN PUBLISHING INC, 4005 W Olympic Blvd, Los Angeles, CA 90019-3258

U.S and Canada Edition © TANTAN PUBLISHING INC in 2015

ISBN: 978-1-939248-04-6

3 4873 00506 3102

All rights reserved. No part of this publication may be reproduced in whole or in part by any means without the prior written permission of TANTAN PUBLISHING INC.

Printed in South Korea at Choil Munhwa Printing Co., 12 Seongsuiro 20 gil, Seongdong-gu, Seoul.

"Could You Lift Up Your Bottom?"

Written by Hee-jung Chang   Illustrated by Sung-hwa Chung

✹TanTan Publishing

Frog was on her way to a friend's house.
She was wearing a fancy hat. Suddenly,
a gust of wind blew her hat away!

A big elephant happened to be passing by and—*PLOP!*
The elephant sat down.

Frog looked as though she was about to cry. She was
sad her favorite hat was under Elephant's bottom.

"Elephant, could you please lift up your bottom?" Frog pleaded.

"I can't because I'm too hungry to move," Elephant said.
"Bring me something good to eat, something . . . **round**."

"Here, Elephant," Frog said. "Eat this **round orange** and then lift up your bottom."

"Humbug!" said Elephant. "An orange won't fill me up. I'm very hungry."

"Bring me something more delicious," Elephant demanded.
"Something shaped like a . . . **triangle**!"

Frog was determined to get her hat back. "Here, Elephant,"
she said. "Eat this delicious sandwich, shaped like a triangle, and
then lift up your bottom."

Activity: Say the name of each of the plane figures out loud: circle, square,
rectangle, and triangle. Find some objects nearby with those shapes.

Elephant was still hungry. "I want something more delicious," he said. "Bring me something shaped like a ... **rectangle**.

Frog had not given up on getting her hat back. "Here," she said.
"Eat this chocolate, shaped like a rectangle, and then lift up your bottom."

But Elephant wouldn't budge. "I won't move until you bring me something even more delicious," he said. "I want something that has a . . . **circle within a circle!**"

Frog was mad. But she was too tiny to push the BIG elephant off of her favorite hat.

Even though she was mad, Frog would not give up. "Here you go," Frog said. "Eat this bagel that is round with a hole in it—and then lift up your bottom!"

"Yum, yum," said Elephant. "That was so delicious!
"But now I want something sweet—something round inside of
something triangular!"

"Phooey!" Frog said. But then she got busy. "Here, hungry elephant," she said. "This ice cream cone has something round inside of something triangular."

Elephant pretended not to notice. "Ho-hum," he said. "There is nothing good to eat. I am going to take a nap." And he did.

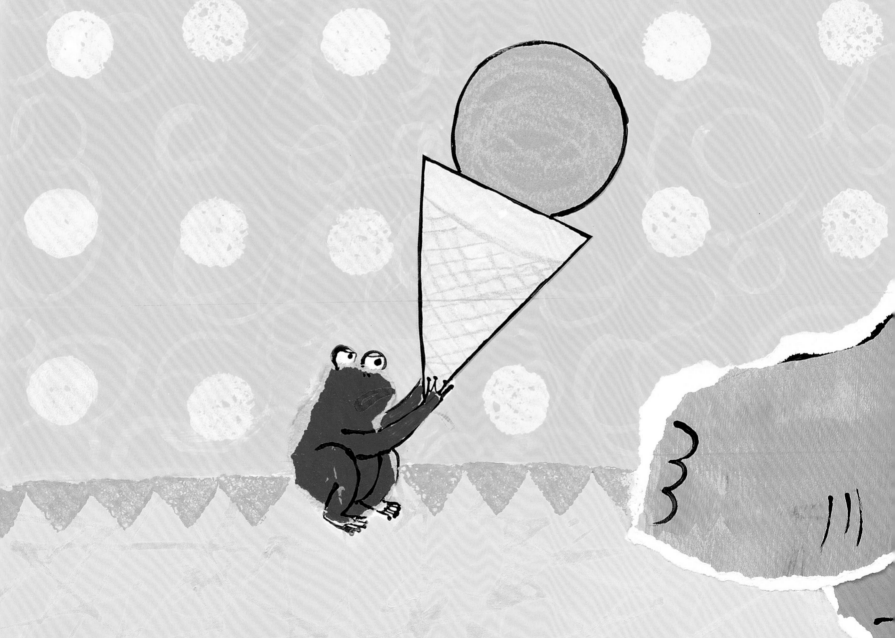

Frog still wanted to get her hat back. "Please!" she pleaded. "Could you kindly lift up your bottom?"

But Elephant was still hungry. "First you must bring me something delicious to eat," he said. "This time I want something with a . . . **special shape**."

The frog came back empty-handed, but she had not
given up on her hat. "Elephant," she said, "I have something
delicious for you! But it is so heavy, I can't bring it to you.
Look—I hung it over there! It's very special."

"Hmmm . . . It looks interesting. What is it?" Elephant asked.

Then Elephant *str-e-e-etched* his long trunk to reach the thing with the special shape—and sucked the sweet honeycomb.

"Yummy—it is delicious!" he said.

But all of sudden—*BUZZZ!*—a swarm of bees attacked the
elephant! He quickly lifted up his bottom and ran for his life.
SPLASH! Elephant plunged into the lake.

And Frog put on her fancy hat and went on her merry way!

Plane Figures in Common Objects

Activities with plane figures are intended to help children:

1. Learn that every object has a shape and that each can be distinguished by its shape.

2. Learn to distinguish objects by recognizing their shapes: circular, triangular, or rectangular.

3. Develop linguistic ability by naming visual shapes with words, for example, saying "circle" when seeing a circular shape. Children who have successfully completed these exercises will have another way of understanding aspects of the world around them.

At this stage, children are not expected to understand the concepts of a line, a plane, and an angle. Nor are they expected to understand the geometry of a circle, a triangle, a square, and a rectangle. They simply should begin to recognize each object's whole shape and connect shapes with familiar words like round, triangular, and rectangular. Encourage children to explore the properties of shapes and express them in words while touching the shapes.

Yum, Yum, Delicious Shapes

| **Activity Goal** | Using food to differentiate and name shapes
| **Materials** | Round crackers, square crackers, bread, butter, jam, slices of ham, slices of cheese,
bread knife, plate, cup

1 On a plate, place the round cracker on top of a slice of cheese. With the bread knife, cut the cheese in the same shape as the cracker, following the edge of the cracker as a guide. Cut the ham in the same way.

2 Have the children put the round cheese and ham in between two round crackers to complete the snacks. Follow the same steps using the square crackers.

3 Cut a slice of bread in half to make two triangle shapes. Using the bread knife, cut the cheese and ham into triangle shapes. Have the children put the triangle-shaped cheese and ham in between the triangular bread slices to complete the sandwiches.

4 Cut the bread into various shapes, such as a circle (using a small cup as a guide), a triangle, or a square. Have the children explore different shapes while spreading butter and jam evenly on each one.

5 Enjoy the food with the children and talk about what other foods have the same shapes.

The grumpy elephant made Frog bring him food in many different shapes. Have fun finding different shapes of food with the clever frog!

Bring me more circle-, triangle-, and rectangle-shaped food!

What are some **circle-shaped** foods?

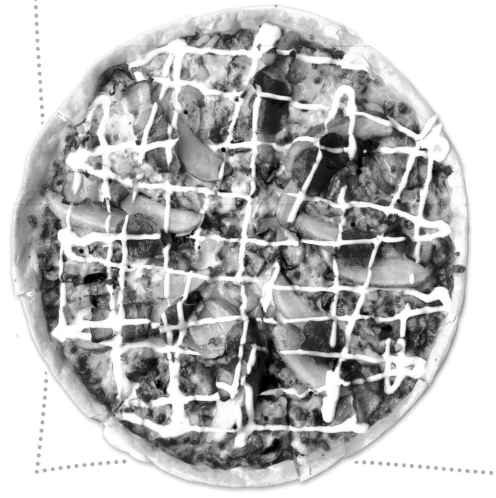

I like the pizza and the cookie.

What are some delicious **triangle-shaped** foods?

Now name some **rectangle-shaped** foods that are tasty!

Many Shapes in a Family

Circular and other **round shapes** are a family. Chubby circles, tall ovals, small ovals, and big circles are all members of the **circle family**.

Triangles are in a family with **pointy shapes**. Small triangles, big triangles, tall triangles, and wide triangles are all members of the **triangle family**.

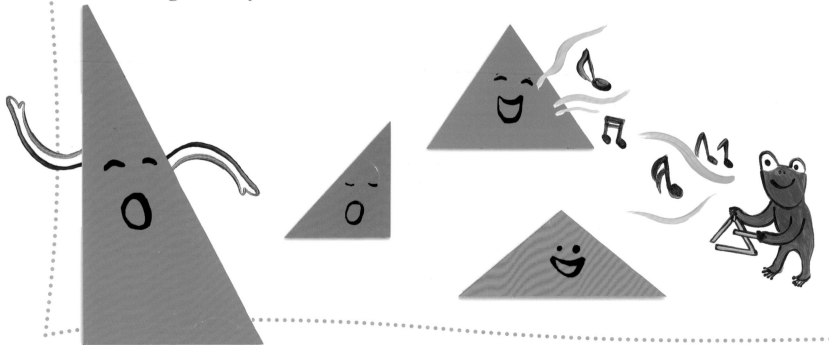

Squares are rectangles. Tall rectangles, tilted squares, wide rectangles, and diamond shapes are all in the **rectangle family**.

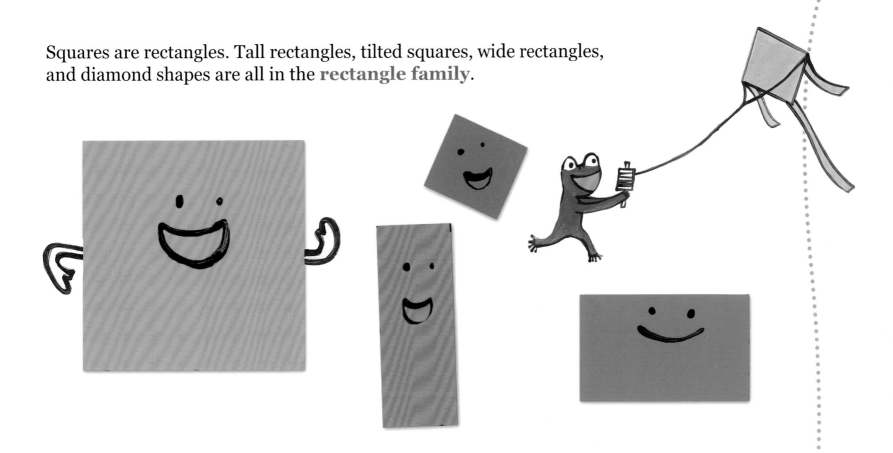

When different shapes connect, new shapes are formed. What shapes can be found in each of the things below?

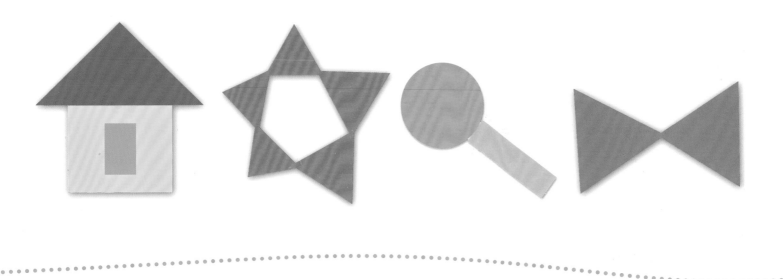